The Biggest Fish in the Lake

**To Benjamin, who got his first lure the day he was born,
and to Dennis, Gary, Tim, David and my brother, John
— with thanks — M.C.**

**To Judy and Clare and the Henderson family,
with great affection and gratitude for their help.
Special thanks to Sophie and to Grandpa Cory — J.W.**

Text © 2001 Margaret Carney
Illustrations © 2001 Janet Wilson

Kids Can Press acknowledges the financial support of the Ontario Arts Council,
the Canada Council for the Arts and the Government of Canada,
through the BPIDP, for our publishing activity.

Published in Canada by
Kids Can Press Ltd.
29 Birch Avenue
Toronto, ON M4V 1E2

Published in the U.S. by
Kids Can Press Ltd.
2250 Military Road
Tonawanda, NY 14150

The artwork in this book was rendered in watercolor.
The text is set in Garth Graphic.

Edited by Tara Walker
Designed by Julia Naimska
Printed and bound in Hong Kong by Book Art Inc., Toronto

This book is smyth sewn casebound.

CM 01 0 9 8 7 6 5 4 3 2 1

Canadian Cataloguing in Publication Data

Carney, Margaret (Margaret Rose), 1947–
The biggest fish in the lake

ISBN 1-55074-720-7

I. Wilson, Janet, 1952– . II. Title.

PS8555.A755B53 2001   jC813'.54   C00-931793-7
PZ7.C37Bi 2001

Kids Can Press is a Nelvana company

The Biggest Fish
in the Lake

Written by **Margaret Carney**
Illustrated by **Janet Wilson**

Kids Can Press

Whenever I'm at Grandpa's farm, and the weather's right and the chores are done, Grandpa and I go fishing.

In spring we fish for speckled trout in the stream running through the pasture. When summer comes, we jig for catfish in the pond. In fall we dangle our lines from the bridge over the river, hoping a fat walleye will grab at our bait. In winter we cut a hole through the ice in the lake and fish for nice big lake trout.

We never know what's lurking in that green underwater world, Grandpa says, or when it will seize our hook. That's half the fun of fishing.

And while we're waiting for a strike, we talk, tell each other stories, or just gaze into the water and listen to the wind. That, Grandpa says, is the best part of all.

I've always used an old bamboo pole to fish, but this year for my birthday I got a huge surprise from Grandpa — a spinning rod of my very own! I hugged him so hard around his whiskery neck that he laughed and said I might strangle him.

"Can we put it together right *now*?" I begged.

Grandpa's eyes twinkled. "Let's see how that reel clamps on there," he answered.

We fitted the rod and reel together, threaded the line through the eyes and tied on a practice plug. Then we hurried out to the barnyard to try it.

My new rod was almost as long as Grandpa's. It felt light and bouncy as I held it like he showed me, swung it back over my shoulder, then flipped it forward. The line went spinning into space.

While I reeled it in and cast again, Grandpa found an old bicycle tire in the woodshed and laid it in the snow. "Try aiming for this," he said. "When you can hit the target two times out of three, I'll give you a lure and we'll go on a fishing trip — for bass."

Bass! Grandpa's best stories were about fishing for bass.

I was so excited that on the very next cast I got my line tangled up in the hedge.

All spring I practiced casting in my backyard in the city. When I went to the farm on weekends, I practiced at the pond.

By the time school was almost out for the summer, I could hit that tire two times out of three, and Grandpa said we should plan our fishing trip. We decided to go at the end of June, on the opening day of bass season.

I could hardly wait.

Finally the big day dawned. After loading our gear into Grandpa's car, we drove a long way north — through deep green woods perfumed with pine, to a cabin on a secluded lake.

The minute we arrived, we carried our fishing tackle down to the dock and fastened a small motor on the boat moored there. We tied silvery lures onto our lines for trolling. Grandpa said the lures would shimmer in the dark water like minnows swimming behind the boat.

As we chugged slowly up the wind-ruffled lake, trailing our lines, we munched on sandwiches and Grandma's chocolate chip cookies.

"Look at that big bird, Grandpa! It's diving!" I cried.

"An osprey, fishing for lunch for its babies," he answered. The osprey flew off with a fat sucker clasped in its claws.

Other birds were fishing, too. As the afternoon sun moved slowly westward, glittering on the waves, we saw a pair of loons, a great blue heron and a kingfisher.

"Where there are fish for birds, there'll be fish for us," Grandpa said.

He caught and released a sunfish and two perch.

All I caught were weeds.

After supper the wind dropped and we headed for some steep rocks along the far shore. From deep black pools, bass were rising for insects, sending rings of ripples across the glassy surface.

Here we used hinged floating lures that jerked like swimming frogs as we reeled them in, a little at a time. I was glad we didn't have to use real frogs.

Before long Grandpa caught a fair-size bass, but he put it back. "If everyone kept all the fish they hooked, there'd be nothing left but little ones," he said. Then Grandpa caught a bigger bass — the perfect size for breakfast.

I was beginning to think I'd never catch a fish when the water near my lure exploded and my rod bent over as if it would break. I yanked up, trying to set the hook, but the big bass that had snapped at my lure leaped in the air and twisted its head, shaking the hook from its mouth.

"Wow, what a whopper!" Grandpa exclaimed. "You almost had a big one."

"Almost" wasn't good enough. I wanted to catch my first bass. I wanted to be just like Grandpa — the greatest fisherman in the world!

We stayed out in the boat till the evening star glimmered over the tips of the dark pines, but we never got another strike. Tired and chilly, we finally headed back to the cabin to bed.

I must have been dreaming about catching a fish, for I woke with a start at dawn. Slipping on my sweater, I went out to the porch without waking Grandpa.

The sky was pearly pink and the air was still. The lake was like smooth gray satin — until all at once, at the end of the dock, a big fish churned the water.

I grabbed my fishing rod and raced down to the shore. Tiptoeing onto the dock, I cast toward where the fish had jumped, and started slowly reeling in my line.

Nothing happened.

I cast to the right and again reeled in.

Taking a deep breath, I cast a third time, toward the weeds near the shore.

With a sudden jerk, my rod flew forward, nearly yanked from my hands. Then my reel was screaming as the line played out. The huge fish had grabbed my lure and was swimming away with it. I could feel the creature's power as it swam — straight toward the weeds, where it could tangle the line and escape.

I planted my feet and pulled back as hard as I could. If I reeled in too quickly, the fish would break the line.

Slowly I wound in a bit, then let the fish swim out. I drew it in again and let it run the other way. Back and forth it darted, tugging on my line, until my arms grew tired.

But the fish was tiring, too.

When I finally reeled it in close enough to glimpse, I almost dropped my rod. This fish wasn't stout and muscular like a bass — it was long and slim, with a narrow snout and sharp teeth.

And it was *big*! It was a muskie!

I didn't have a net, so I carefully drew the muskie along the dock toward shore, keeping tension on the line like Grandpa taught me. When I got the fish to the shallows, I jumped into the water right behind it.

With a flip of its tail, the muskie leaped away toward the beach. Half in and half out of the water, it lay on its side, panting.

Heart pounding, I stared in wonder at the fish, from its glaring eye to its long fanned tail. I couldn't wait to show it to Grandpa. He'd be so proud of me! I had caught the biggest fish in the lake — a mighty muskie!

One scoop of my arms could land it. I bent forward, then froze. The muskie was so magnificent — so powerful and sleek.

Suddenly I wasn't sure I wanted to keep it.

But the hook had pierced the muskie's mouth, and its teeth looked razor sharp. How could I free the barb without getting cut? When I reached out to try, the fish thrashed, and I jumped in fright.

If I got it up on shore, I might be able to free it. I was just bending down again when, with a powerful surge, the muskie snapped the line, leaped toward open water and was gone. I fell back with a splash.

It was only then that I noticed Grandpa. He was silhouetted against the sunrise, watching me.

"I caught a big fish, Grandpa!" I called out breathlessly. "It wasn't a bass, it was a muskie. But I — I had to let it go."

Grandpa nodded. Then he smiled and started toward me. "They put up quite a fight, don't they? Muskies are a whole lot of fish to handle."

Instead of stopping at the shoreline, Grandpa walked straight into the water and caught me up in a hug, dripping clothes and all. "After so much excitement, I'll bet you're hungry. How about I fry up those bass fillets while you dry off and tell me all about your muskie?"

I hugged Grandpa back, burying my face in his warm flannel shirt. Then I grinned at him.

"Bass for breakfast? Let's eat!" I said. "Then let's go see what else is lurking in the lake."